"I am happy to endorse *A Girl Like Tilly*. Girls with ASD are looking for books based on personal experiences so that they can share and contrast their feelings with others. The age range for this group is particularly needed."

Professor Gillian Baird OBE, Vice President of the National Autistic Society, Vice President of Afasic and consultant in children's neurodisability

•

"A charming tale about a little girl, which also features the narratives of Mum, Grandma, Teacher and Psychologist. Although autism is different in everyone, Tilly strongly resonated with me. I also like how timely the story is, as it mentions how the world is 'learning more now about what autism looks like in girls'. A sweet, charming story that has been enhanced with hand-drawn illustrations."

Alis Rowe, Entrepreneur and Founder of *The Curly Hair Project*

•

"*A Girl Like Tilly* is a lovely story highlighting a girl's journey with autism from birth through her school years. Tilly is like many girls I see in my practice – bright and gifted but socially confused and anxious, who is trying to find her place in a neurotypical world."

Danuta Bulhak-Paterson, Clinical Psychologist and author of *I am an Aspie Girl: A book for young girls with autism spectrum conditions*

•

"I absolutely loved this book. It is so beautifully illustrated and visually gives such a sense of Tilly's world. We see so many small details of her life and learn why she is who she is. An informative, realistic yet positive read for all autistic girls and their families."

Sarah Hendrickx, autistic adult and author of *Women and Girls with Autism Spectrum Disorder*

•

"Anyone working with girls on the spectrum will treasure this book! It is easy to read and therefore suitable for children too. It provides very descriptive and well-presented information about how it is to be a girl on a spectrum. Ellen Li's illustrations are excellent and accompany the text in a great manner."

Despina Giza, Med In Special Education Needs, Autism

•

"As someone who was once a girl very much like Tilly, I found the main character's journey relatable and her reactions spot on. For girls who are just discovering that they are on the spectrum, Tilly's story is both an icebreaker and a comforting reassurance that there are other girls just like them."

Cynthia Kim, author of *Nerdy, Shy and Socially Inappropriate: A User Guide to an Asperger Life*

•

This book was written as a testament to a young
woman's courage and to honour her experiences.

It is for girls and women, their families, friends
and carers where autism is a concern.

It is also for those professionals who seek to better
understand the nature of female autism.

A Girl Like Tilly

Growing up with Autism

Helen Bates

Illustrated by Ellen Li

Jessica Kingsley *Publishers*
London and Philadelphia

Everyone agrees that Tilly is a lovely baby.

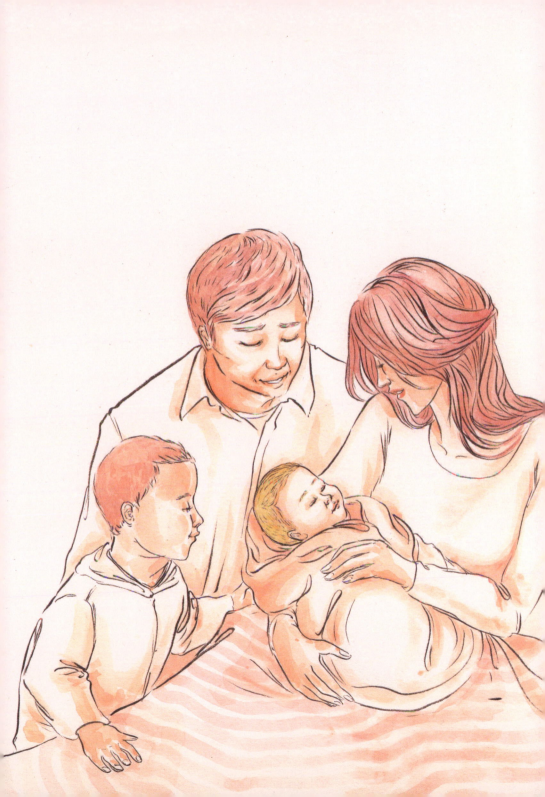

But, like all new arrivals, she keeps everyone on their toes.

"Mmmmm," says Mum, "Tilly really doesn't like to be
on her own but she's not too keen on cuddling either."

Grandad is taking photos.

"She's lost in her daydreams again," says Grandma.

"I think she likes her very own secret world best," says big brother Tim.

"I'll jolly her along," says Grandad. "I'll give her a big hug."

But Tilly has already run away.

"Never mind," says Grandma. "I expect you're a bit prickly. I think she'd like to go tadpoling with you instead."

Tilly is learning about lots of things very quickly. Everyone thinks she is very clever and will love going to school. She can remember the names of all her brother's toy cars.

Ford Cortina

mini cooper

fiat

vw Beetle

But when will she learn to ride her bike?

or tie her shoe laces?

or button up her coat?

or catch a ball?

or use her knife and folk?

However, when she starts school, Tilly doesn't like it at all. She would much rather be at home with Mum, where everything is safe and she knows what's what. School is all new and strange and there's lots of noise and funny smells. In fact, it's rather frightening.

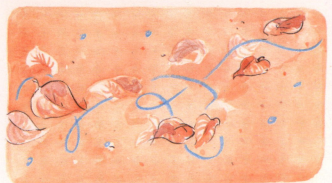

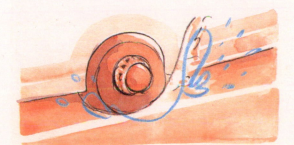

"She's just Little Miss Shy," says the teacher.

"Oh dear," say Mum and Dad, "Tilly isn't doing very well at school after all. But just see how quickly she has made this model boat."

"And sorted out my flat pack," says Dad.

"Oh dear," says the teacher, "Tilly has been on the same page of this book for weeks. Whatever shall we do?"

"Still daydreaming," say Mum, Dad, Grandma and Grandad.

And it's true. Tilly has a secret world to escape to with her make-believe friend Simon. Mum thinks she's too big for Simon now, but they have such good times together in the special land Tilly makes out of toy bricks and modelling clay – and her imagination. And the best thing is that she can go there any time she likes.

"She does love to tell me stories about everything that happens at home," says the teacher.

"By the way, I do hope you can make it up with your best friend," she whispers to Mum.

Tilly finds it very difficult to know what it's OK to talk about and what is private (and she can be very blunt).

So what does Tilly **like** to do?

Well, best of all Tilly loves spending time with her black cat Gilbert. He is always ready for a chat. She tells him everything and he seems to understand that Tilly's life is quite difficult.

She just can't seem to get the hang of it like other children can. It seems very easy to get everything wrong. But she thinks that if she copies what they do she will learn to be like them. So that's what she tries to do.

She wishes that everyone else was as understanding as Gilbert. Maybe she just wasn't in the right place when someone was explaining how to work it all out.

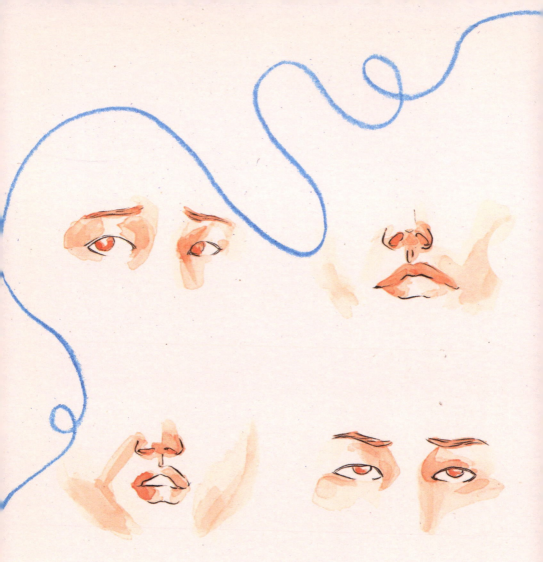

And Tilly loves to tell the other children about Gilbert.
But sometimes the children don't seem to want to listen any more.
They look bored but Tilly doesn't notice. They want to talk about
other things and get cross when Tilly keeps butting in.

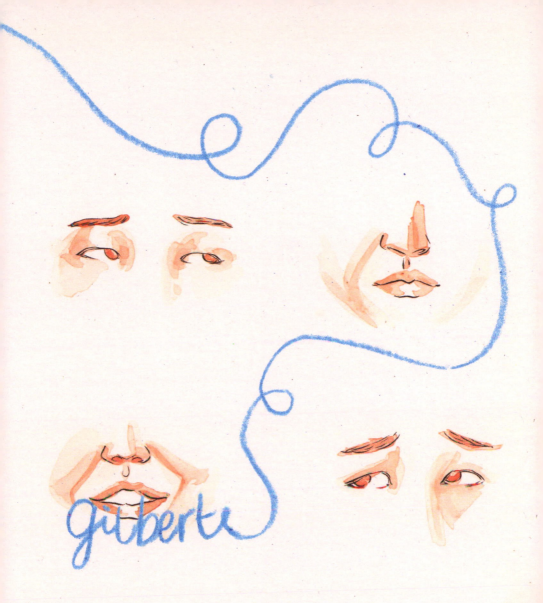

Tilly realises that there must be a lot of rules about conversations.

"However will I be able to learn them all?" she wonders.

It's such hard work trying to get things right. It makes Tilly feel very anxious and tired.

But sometimes it really doesn't matter.

Hooray! Tilly feels very safe with her Mum's best friend Mary and can join in the running and jumping and chasing and ball-kicking with Sam, Ben and big brother Tim.

She can just be Tilly and not worry about making mistakes, like her fun times riding her little pony Bramble every Sunday morning, and going to the pool with Dad and Tim.

The little girls always invite Tilly to their parties.

But she will not go – **not ever.**

Mum, there are things I want to tell you but I don't know how.

I hate wearing a dress.

I like to have my tea at home.

And I won't stay here because I want to be in my own home.

In fact, Tilly seems to be happier when she's with the grown-ups. She's been listening carefully to how they talk to each other.

"Tilly is very polite and charming," they say.

Tilly finds grown-ups a bit more predictable.

Perhaps she could invite them all to her birthday party?

Hello.

How are you?

I'm so pleased you could make it.

Isn't the weather nice?

"Oh, I don't think so," says Mum.

"But if you don't want a party we'll think of a nice surprise treat."

"**NO**," says Tilly, "I don't like surprises. I like things to be the same. I get cross when you make my bed and move my teddies.

And I get cross when you interrupt me when I'm checking things.

And when you try to hurry me up at bedtime."

"Well, I get cross too," says Mum. "You take such a long time."

"And I worry a lot when I can't wear my favourite jumper,"

says Tilly, stamping her foot.

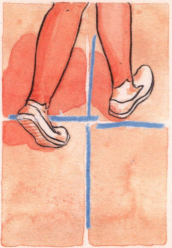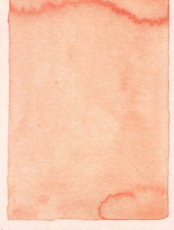
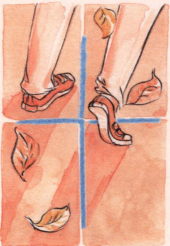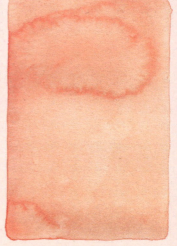
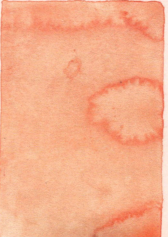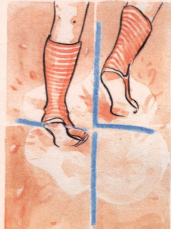

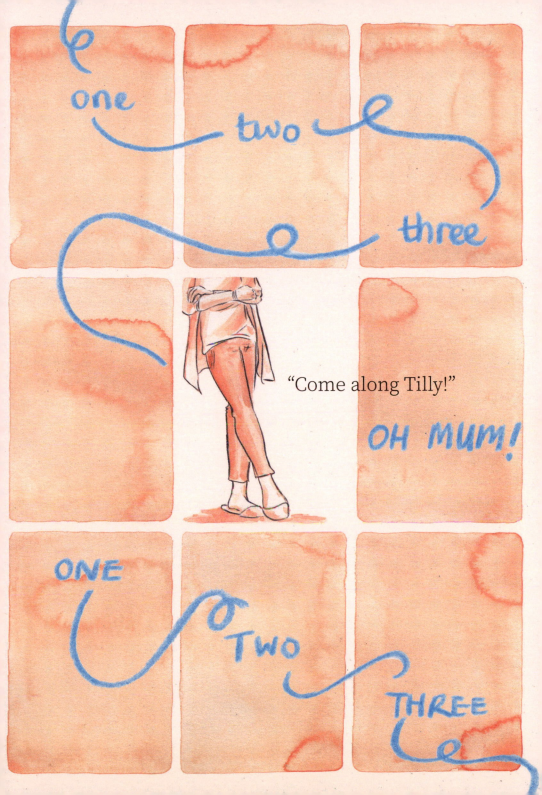

The psychologist says, "Tilly is bright as a button, but reading and writing are a big worry for her."

So off she goes to see Gemma, a special teacher, for some English lessons all by herself. She looks forward to Tuesdays coming round.

"Phew," say Mum and Dad, "it's good to have that sorted out at last!"

But is it?

Tilly's not so sure.

She is trying to do her best but the world seems to be an even more mysterious and bewildering place as she is getting older.

How do other people manage to cope?

Especially at school.

Sad to say it can be so very difficult that Tilly just stops trying. Sometimes she daydreams or talks to herself. She has even been known to sing – and not particularly quietly.

And that means she's in trouble **again**.

Worst of all, nothing ever stays the same.

Nowadays the other girls **never** want to hear about Gilbert at all.

They talk about their hair and clothes all the time and squeal and giggle a lot.

And when boys are around they behave in ways that are very puzzling to Tilly.

"Oh dear,"

says Mum, having a little cry.
"I sometimes feel at my wits' end.
I love Tilly very much, she is a very special
daughter. But she seems to be a bit stuck."

"Don't worry," says Mary.
"She's a regular tomboy, but it's just a
phase. She's so pretty, just you wait."

Tilly isn't sure what Mary is waiting for!

Tilly knows she doesn't feel comfortable in her
own skin. She even sometimes asks herself,

"Am I a girl? Am I a boy?"

"I guess I'm a Tilly," she thinks, "but being a Tilly
is very confusing indeed."

"Oh dear,"

says Dad, shedding a little tear, "the other
girls are leaving Tilly behind. She just
doesn't seem interested in growing up."

Mum and Dad are so worried because Tilly seems very unhappy sometimes.

She wakes up in the night. Sometimes she has a bad tummy ache.

She is not able to put how she feels into words, so no one knows about how the other girls treat her.

Sometimes they steal her lunch and call her stupid.

But it would never, ever cross Tilly's mind to not go to school every day, no matter how horrid it is. She is very dutiful and conscientious...

But every day is such a struggle.

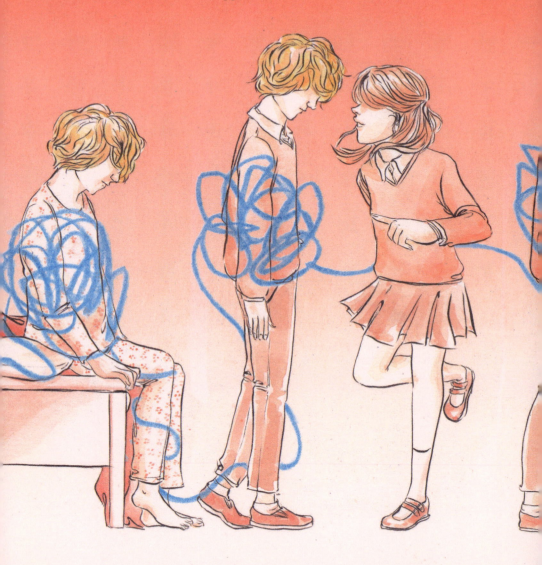

Tilly feels as if she has to start from the very
beginning, all over again, every morning.

Now Grandma has something important to say. Grandma is Tilly's most favourite person. Somehow she seems to have always understood. She gives Tilly a feeling she doesn't have with anyone else. Grandma says she keeps her in mind even when she's far away. Tilly likes this idea very much, although she finds it hard to imagine.

"My dearest Tilly. I have been doing a lot of wondering and reading and I think that we should all go and see the nice psychologist again. I believe you'll find out what makes you special."

social understanding

communication

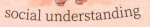

routines and rituals

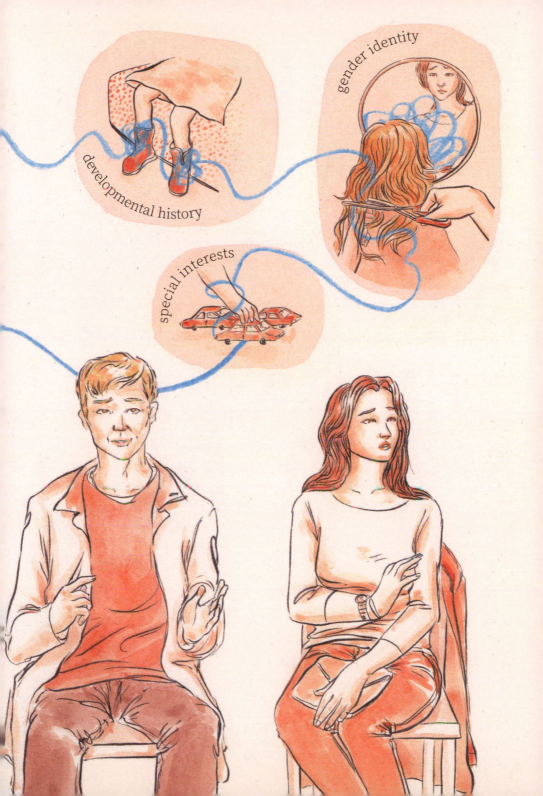

"Tilly, I'm very sorry it has taken so long for us to understand the things you find so difficult about your life. I am glad that we are learning more now about what autism looks like in girls as well as boys, so that we can help sooner. I can see that it's been really hard work and you are quite worn out by trying to puzzle it all out by yourself. But Tilly, while you've been growing up the world has changed for girls like you. You have something different and important to offer."

"So what happens now?" ask Mum, Dad, Grandma and
Grandad – and her teacher.

"We all want to help Tilly as much as we can.
How do we do that?"

"Well," says Grandma, "I think the best person to tell us that is Tilly herself. She has lots of hopes and dreams, you know. But we've all been so tied up with the problems, like knots in a rope, that we haven't been able to find out about them. We are setting out on a new journey now."

"I am Tilly. I have autism and that makes me different. It does help to have a reason for everything that's happened and to know that there are other girls with autism too. But no one is quite like me and we don't all have the same story.

Now I'm starting to understand myself better there are things I would like some help with. I would really like to learn some rules for when I'm with people – what's OK and what's not OK. Can I say 'no' sometimes? How do I let people know what I'm feeling? I can't find the right words even when it's very important. I often feel so bad and I worry a lot about growing up and keeping myself safe. How can I learn to be more confident and find a place where I belong?"

"I am Tilly. I have autism. But that's not all you should know about me! I love history. I love music. I love computer games. I make good jokes and bake good cakes. I love playing hockey. I really want to be an archaeologist one day. And I really, really want to ride a motorbike."

Not all journeys are the same,
or as lonely and long.

Although being different can bring problems,
maybe it can also lead to possibilities.

Further Reading and Resources

There are many books and resources providing information about autism, although not yet many that are specifically about and for girls and women. Adults and young people will be able to choose which resources best fit their needs, and parents and carers will work out which are most suitable for their child. Reading together is not only a great family activity but also helps everyone to share experiences, hopes and concerns and increase their understanding.

Books for children and young people

My Sister is Different
Author & illustrator: Sarah Tamsin-Hunter (2006)
Published by The National Autistic Society

My Family is Different: A Workbook for Children with a Brother or Sister on the Autistic Spectrum
Author: Carolyn Brock (2007)
Published by The National Autistic Society

The ASD Workbook: Understanding Your Autistic Spectrum Disorder
Author: Penny Kershaw (2011)
Published by Jessica Kingsley Publishers

I am an Aspie Girl: A book for young girls with autistic spectrum conditions
Author: Danuta Bulhak-Paterson
Illustrator: Teresa Ferguson (2015)
Published by Jessica Kingsley Publishers

Books for parents and carers

The Autistic Spectrum: A Parent's Guide
Author: The National Autistic Society
Published by The National Autistic Society

Parenting Girls on the Autistic Spectrum: Overcoming the Challenges and Celebrating the Gifts
Author: Eileen Riley-Hall (2012)
Published by Jessica Kingsley Publishers

Autism: Supporting Your Teenager
Author: Caroline Hattersley (2014)
Published by The National Autistic Society

Books for adults

The Way I See It: A Personal Look at Autism and Asperger's
Author: Temple Grandin (2015)
Published by Future Horizons, Inc.

Women and Girls with Autism Spectrum Disorder: Understanding Life Experiences from Early Childhood to Old Age
Author: Sarah Hendricks (2015)
Published by Jessica Kingsley Publishers

Asperger's and Girls: World-Renowned Experts Join Those with Asperger's Syndrome to Resolve Issues that Girls and Women Face Every Day
Editors: Tony Attwood & Temple Grandin (2006)
Published by EDS Publications Ltd.

I am an Aspie Woman: The Unique Characteristics, Traits and Gifts of Adult Females on the Autistic Spectrum
Author: Tania Marshall (2015)
Published by Aspiengirl

Thinking in Pictures
Author: Temple Grandin (2006)
Published by Random House

Aspergirls: Empowering Females with Asperger Syndrome
Author: Rudy Simone (2010)
Published by Jessica Kingsley Publishers

Books for professionals

*The Autistic Spectrum: A Guide
for Parents and Professionals*
Author: Lorna Wing (2003)
Published by Robinson

*Mental Health and Autism: A Guide for Child
and Adolescent Mental Health Practitioners*
Author: Patrick Sims (2011)
Published by The National Autistic Society

*Educating and Supporting Girls with
Asperger's and Autism: A Resource for
Education and Health Professionals*
Author: Victoria Honeybourne (2016)
Published by Speechmark Publishing Ltd.

International not-for-profit groups across the world offering help and support for people affected by ASD

United Kingdom	www.autism.org.uk
Ireland	www.autismireland.ie
USA	www.autism-society.org
Canada	www.autismsocietycanada.ca
Australia	www.autismaus.com.au
New Zealand	www.autism.org.nz

Websites and blogs

http://autisminpink.net
An EU-funded partnership between four
European organisations, which has been set
up to carry out research into autism in women.
Breaking the Silence online book available.

www.autismeducationtrust.org.uk
Provides examples of good practice,
practical toolkits and resources for
families and professionals.

www.autism.org.uk
Providing information, support and services.

http://thegirlwiththecurlyhair.co.uk
The curly haired project.

https://dinahtheaspiedinosaur.wordpress.com
Dinah the aspie dinosaur.

www.incentiveplus.co.uk
Innovative social, emotional, behavioural,
mental health and wellbeing resources.

DVDs

Being Me (DVD and CD-ROM)
Author: NAS (2008)

A Different Life: Rosie's Story (DVD)
Author: Eye Television (2006)

Also of interest

*The Reason I Jump: One Boy's Voice
from the Silence of Autism*
Author: Naoki Higashida
Translators: David Mitchell & Keiko Yoshida (2014)
Published by Sceptre

The Curious Incident of the Dog in the Night-time
Author: Mark Haddon (2003)
Published by David Fickling Books

On the Edge of Gone
Author: Corinne Duyvis (2016)
Published by Amulet Books

Acknowledgements

This is a wonderful opportunity to say thank you to the many friends, relatives and professionals who have supported Rachel and her family over the years.

My grateful thanks to Susan Potter and Sarah Temple, without whom I would never have had the privilege of my collaboration and friendship with Ellen. Through her insight, sensitivity, imagination and skill she has brought Tilly's thoughts and feelings vividly to life, making the invisible visible. My thanks to her are inestimable.

Thank you also to Rosie Barnes for her generous interest and support.

Our dearest family, Jonathan, Shiho and Amy, have inspired through their determination and resilience in surmounting challenges in their own lives, and have brought us much joy.

David has always given his committed and enthusiastic support and provided a secure, caring base from which to revisit the past.

We have greatly appreciated the encouragement and thoughtful guidance from Jessica Kingsley and also wish to thank her staff, especially Emily, Daisy and Victoria, for their invaluable contribution.

And, finally, my special gratitude to Rachel for sharing her story and for a life which touches so many – sometimes with sadness and pain but always with humour, intelligence, honesty and love.